YOU and ME and HOME SWEET HOME

George Ella Lyon & Stephanie Anderson

A RICHARD JACKSON BOOK
Atheneum Books for Young Readers
New York • London • Toronto • Sydney

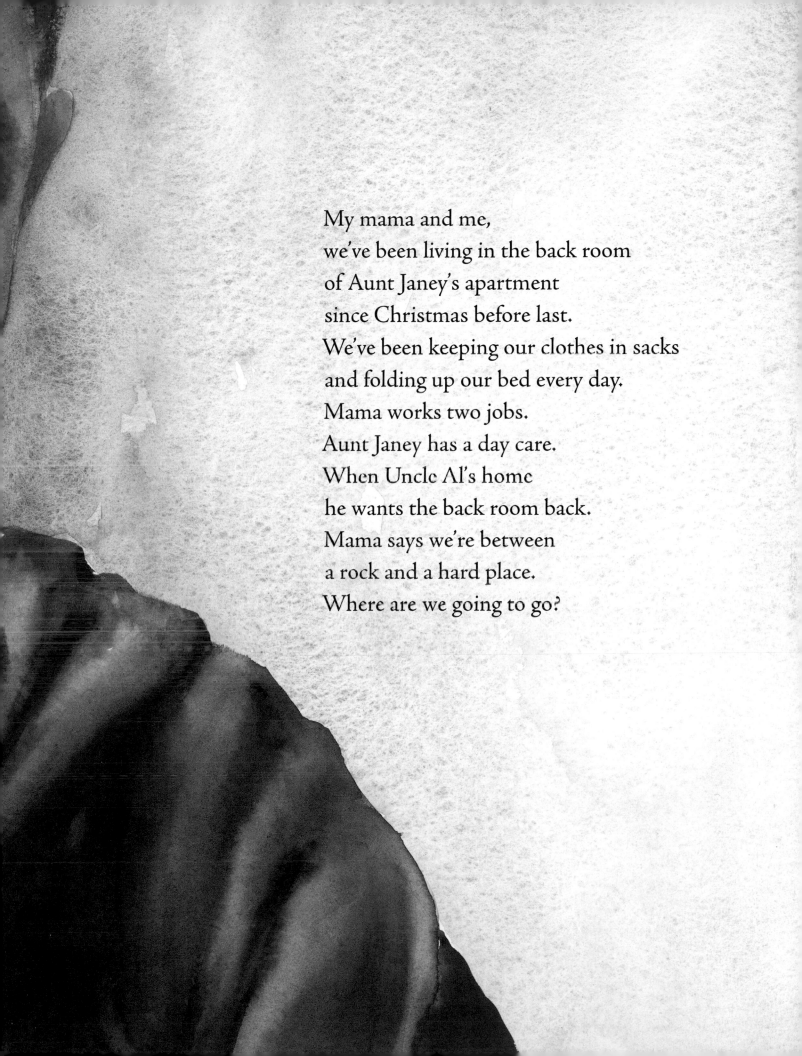

My mama and me,
we've been living in the back room
of Aunt Janey's apartment
since Christmas before last.
We've been keeping our clothes in sacks
and folding up our bed every day.
Mama works two jobs.
Aunt Janey has a day care.
When Uncle Al's home
he wants the back room back.
Mama says we're between
a rock and a hard place.
Where are we going to go?

Then people from the church,
Brother Felix and Sister Clara,
they say they know where.
They say our church family
is going to build us a house.
"Right," I say. Like I'm going
to tap-dance on the moon.

"Lots of people will help," Mama says.
"And we'll work on it, too.
Our house will be stronger
if we help build it."

A couple of months later
Mama takes me to see
the place where our house will be.
"That's nothing," I say.
"That's just a little plot of grass."
"That's all we need," Mama says back.
"A little land, a lot of faith,
and people come to help."

"What about wood?" I ask.
"Don't we need wood?"
She smiles. "I forgot that," she says.

Finally in the fall
building day comes.
All kinds of folks show up,
not just ones from church—
young and old, black and white.
Some wear tool belts
and know what they are doing.
Others need practice to hit a nail.

Our leader, Diane, says we'll work
this house like a puzzle.
"Do you mean me?" I ask.
"Can I build too?"
"Kids aren't allowed
to work construction," Diane says.

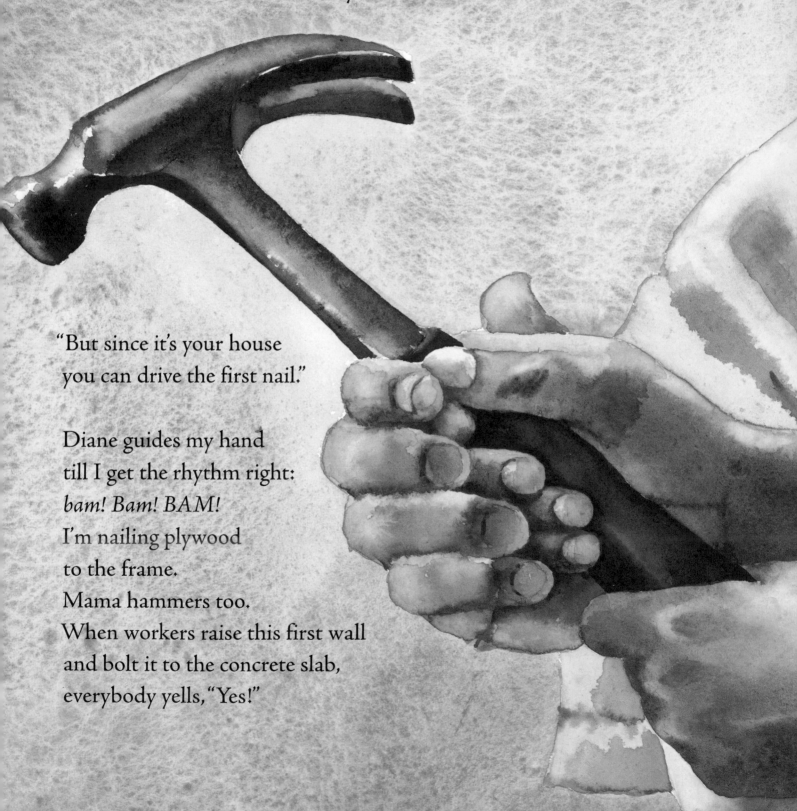

"But since it's your house
you can drive the first nail."

Diane guides my hand
till I get the rhythm right:
bam! Bam! BAM!
I'm nailing plywood
to the frame.
Mama hammers too.
When workers raise this first wall
and bolt it to the concrete slab,
everybody yells, "Yes!"

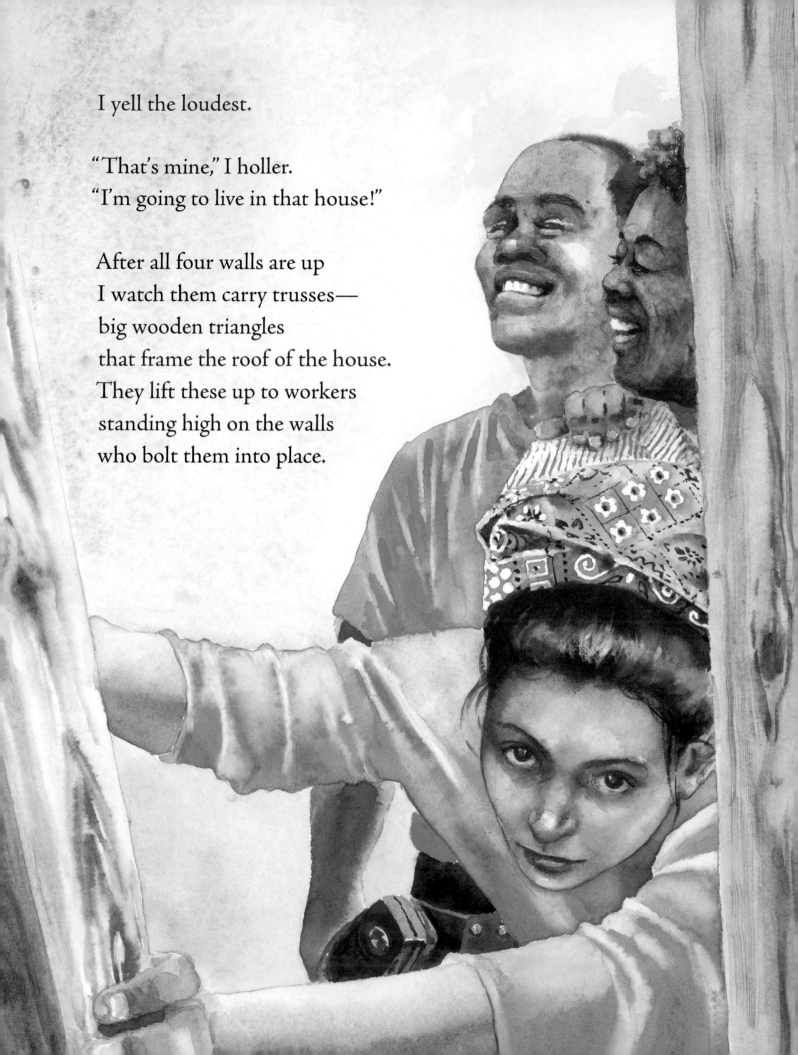

I yell the loudest.

"That's mine," I holler.
"I'm going to live in that house!"

After all four walls are up
I watch them carry trusses—
big wooden triangles
that frame the roof of the house.
They lift these up to workers
standing high on the walls
who bolt them into place.

When I get tired of watching
I go hunt for Diane.
She's bent over a big saw.
"I want to help too," I tell her.
"What can I do?"

Diane looks up and smiles.
"Whoa! Stay clear of the saw!"
She takes off her safety glasses.
"It's your house," she says.
"You can build a window box
for the front porch."

A woman named Rita helps me.
She saws the pieces
then holds them in place
while I hammer.
bam! Bam! BAM!
Come spring our windows will bloom.

By the time I'm finished,
the roof trusses are all set
and the sun pours through.
I do a "Love Your Roof" dance.

"Done for the day!" Diane shouts.
Workers climb down
and put away tools.

But before we leave
we all stand and look.
This morning there was
nothing but a concrete slab.
Now there's the whole shape
of our house. Sweet!

On the ride to Aunt Janey's
  I ask Mama,
"Can I skip school tomorrow
and keep working on our house?"

"Child," Mama says, "you must have
hit your head with that hammer.
School is your job. I go to work,
you go to work. Other folks
will keep building the house."
"But Mama—"
"*After* school you can help."

Next morning I tell my teacher
about hammering the first nail.
"That is fabulous!" Miss Bliss says.
"Class, listen up. Sharonda is building a house."
I feel so tall then.
Also my heart is glowing.
"Not a *real* house," Denny Sizemore says.
"Not a house you live in."
"It is, too," I tell him.
"It's already got walls and roof trusses."
Miss Bliss sends me to the board
to draw and explain.
Wait'll I tell Mama I'm educating
the whole third grade.

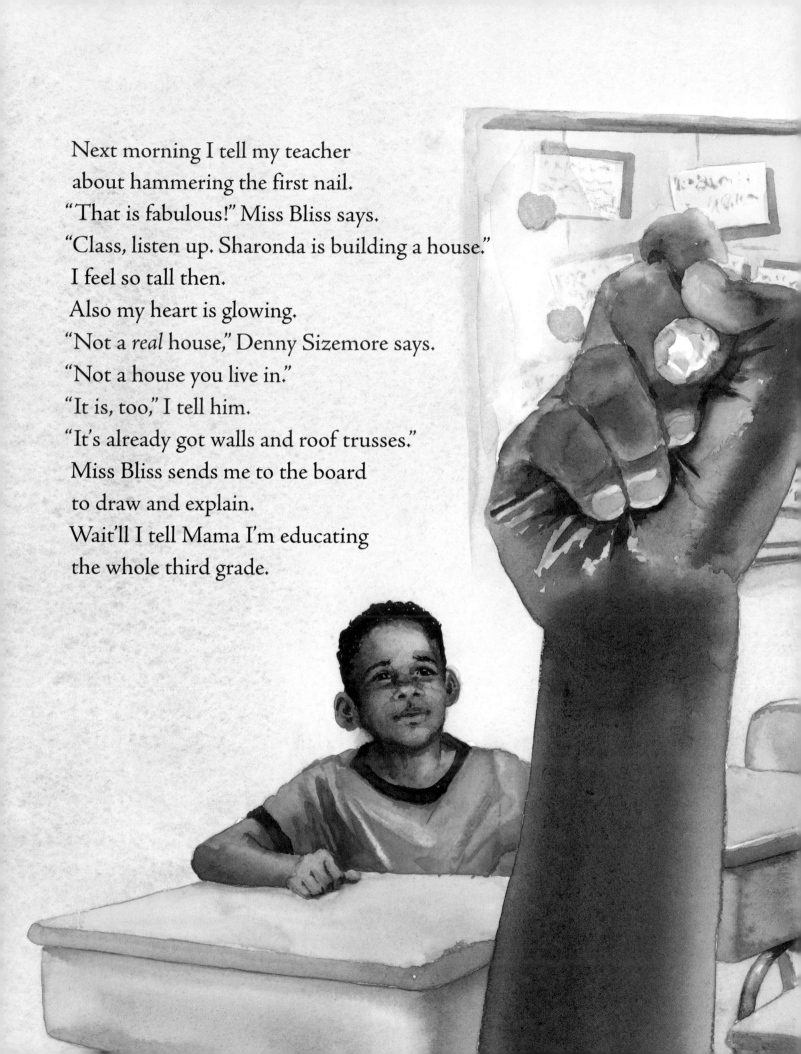

That afternoon I have a pass
to ride a different bus—
not the one to Aunt Janey's,
the one that goes to *my* house.
I see it as soon as we turn the corner—
walls all blue and silver
(that's the insulation)
and look! There's wood
over the trusses!
It won't rain in my room now!

I walk around to see what they've done.
Some folks have started
to put the siding on.
Diane says she's glad I'm here.
The afternoon is hot
and I can hand out water bottles.
"It's your house," she says.
"You've got to water these workers
to make it grow."
I grab an armful of bottles
and head out. Diane calls, "Sharonda!
Not so close to the ladder!"

And that is how it goes.
All week while I'm working
    at school,
folks are measuring, sawing,
drilling and hammering
to build me and Mama a house.
All week I go there
    after school to help.

Once it's roofed in
they call in the experts —
the ones that put in pipes
    and wires
and inspect it all to make sure
    it's right.

I arrive just as they're finishing up
    and Diane has me sweep out the trash.
"I know," I tell her. "It's my house."

When they leave, we have a pizza party.
We hold hands around a card table
in the backyard of my house
and Sister Clara prays:

God our Maker
bless this food and work.
Use our hands
to build a better world.
                    Amen

I brush sawdust off my pizza and dig in.

The next day workers put up drywall
and hang windows and doors.
Brother Felix hands out brushes
and buckets of paint.
Diane promised I could paint
the window boxes while Mama
helps paint my room.
I've got an old T-shirt
in my backpack
so as soon as I get off the bus
I'm ready to work. It goes
on smooth, this delicious color.
I paint to the rhythm
of shingles nailed on the roof.

Finally the last day comes.
Workers lay the carpet,
put in the toilets and sinks.
By the time I get there,
it is a house—
a real live house!

"Can we stay here
    tonight?"
I ask Mama.

"Hold your horses," she says.
"Tomorrow's the dedication.
Then we move in."

So I wait. I curl up one last night
in the pull-out bed at Aunt Janey's.

The next day about noon
a crowd fills our yard.
Mama and I stand on the porch
beside Sister Clara. Somebody sings,
Brother Felix prays.
Diane hands me the hammer
I used to drive the first nail.
There's a little sign on it now
with our name and address.
She gives Mama the keys.
"Welcome to your house," she says.
Everybody cheers.

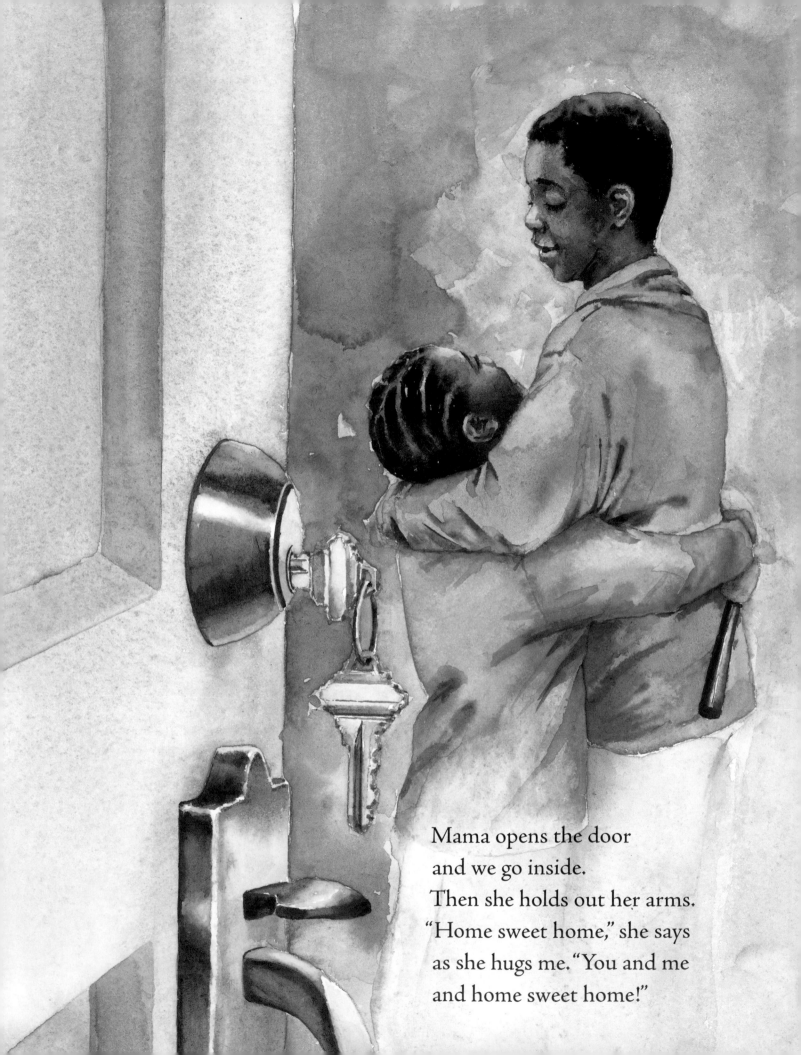

Mama opens the door
and we go inside.
Then she holds out her arms.
"Home sweet home," she says
as she hugs me. "You and me
and home sweet home!"

For Diane, Jean, Cheryl, Sharonda, and Ann

For all who use their hands to build a better world

In memory of my grandfather, Robert Hoskins Sr.,
who built the house I grew up in

　　　　　　　　　　— G. E. L.

　　　　　　　　　For Gramma and Grampa
　　　　　　　　　and for Steve　　　　　　*S. A.*

AUTHOR'S NOTE

You and Me and Home Sweet Home grew out of a Women's Build I worked on in Lexington, Kentucky, in September of 2000. My thanks to all involved, especially Diane James.

———

Atheneum Books for Young Readers ◆ An imprint of Simon & Schuster Children's Publishing Division ◆ 1230 Avenue of the Americas, New York, New York 10020 ◆ Text copyright © 2009 by George Ella Lyon ◆ Illustrations copyright © 2009 by Stephanie Anderson ◆ All rights reserved, including the right of reproduction in whole or in part in any form. ◆ Book design by Ann Bobco ◆ The text for this book is set in Adobe Jenson. ◆ The illustrations for this book are rendered in watercolor with pastel pencil. ◆ Manufactured in China ◆ First Edition ◆ 10 9 8 7 6 5 4 3 2 1 ◆ Library of Congress Cataloging-in-Publication Data ◆ Lyon, George Ella, 1949– ◆ You and me and home sweet home / George Ella Lyon ; illustrated by Stephanie Anderson. — 1st ed. ◆ p.　cm. ◆ "A Richard Jackson book." ◆ Summary: Third-grader Sharonda and her mother help volunteers from their church and their community to build the house that will be their very own. ◆ ISBN: 978-0-689-87589-2 ◆ [1. House construction—Fiction. 2. Building—Fiction. 3. Voluntarism—Fiction. 4. African Americans—Fiction.] I. Anderson, Stephanie, 1976– ill. II. Title. ◆ PZ7.L9954You 2009 ◆ [E]—dc22 ◆ 2008010414